Dear Parents and Educators,

Welcome to Penguin Young Readers! As parents and educators, you
know that each child develops at his or her own pace—in terms of
speech, critical thinking, and, of course, reading. Penguin Young Readers
recognizes this fact. As a result, each Penguin Young Readers book is
assigned a traditional easy-to-read level (1–4) as well as a
Guided Reading Level (A–P). Both of these systems will help you choose
the right book for your child. Please refer to the back of each book
for specific leveling information. Penguin Young Readers features
esteemed authors and illustrators, stories about favorite characters,
fascinating nonfiction, and more!

## The Barker Twins™: T-Rex Is Missing!

LEVEL **2**

GUIDED
READING
LEVEL **H**

This book is perfect for a **Progressing Reader** who:
- can figure out unknown words by using picture and context clues;
- can recognize beginning, middle, and ending sounds;
- can make and confirm predictions about what will happen in the text; and
- can distinguish between fiction and nonfiction.

Here are some **activities** you can do during and after reading this book:
- Problem/Solution: This story has a problem—Morgie's dinosaur is missing.
  Discuss why this is a problem. Then talk about how the problem is solved.
- Sight Words: Sight words are frequently used words that readers must
  know just by looking at them. These words are known instantly, on sight.
  Knowing these words helps children develop into efficient readers. The
  sight words listed below appear in this book. As you read the story,
  point out the sight words.

| after | better | found | over | under |
|-------|--------|-------|----------|-------|
| again | came | I'm | thought | were |
| always | didn't | next | together | where |

Remember, sharing the love of reading with a child is the best gift
you can give!

—Bonnie Bader, EdM
  Penguin Young Readers program

*Penguin Young Readers are leveled by independent reviewers applying the standards developed by Irene Fountas
and Gay Su Pinnell in *Matching Books to Readers: Using Leveled Books in Guided Reading*, Heinemann, 1999.

For Morgie and Moffie's friends, Dr. Cheryl
and Dr. Ken Schunk and their staff at the
Hillsborough County Veterinary Hospital . . . and
for Mario who has never had a T-Rex missing!

Jennifer Smith-Stead, Literacy Consultant

PENGUIN YOUNG READERS
An Imprint of Penguin Random House LLC

Copyright © 2002 by Tomie dePaola. All rights reserved. First published in 2002 by Grosset & Dunlap,
an imprint of Penguin Random House LLC. THE BARKER TWINS is a trademark of
Penguin Random House LLC. Published in 2012 by Penguin Young Readers, an imprint of
Penguin Random House LLC, 345 Hudson Street, New York, New York 10014. Manufactured in China

Library of Congress Control Number: 2002004661

ISBN 9780448428703                                    10 9 8 7 6 5 4 3

PENGUIN YOUNG READERS

Level 2

PROGRESSING READER

# THE BARKER TWINS

# T-REX IS MISSING!

by Tomie dePaola

Penguin Young Readers
An Imprint of Penguin Random House

"Steggie, Steggie.

Come here," T-Rex said.

"Gotcha! It's my cave now."

"You mean *again*," Billy said.

"T-Rex always wins."

Billy asked, "How come you are always T-Rex?"

"Because he's my favorite," Morgie answered.

Just then, Mama called Morgie.

"Come and get some snacks.

Billy has to go home soon."

"Okay, Mama," Morgie called.

"I'm coming."

Morgie came back.

Billy was packing up

his backpack.

They had snacks.

Then Billy went home.

After dinner, Morgie

got ready for bed.

He counted his dinosaurs.

Oh no! T-Rex was missing!

Morgie looked all over—

under the bed,

in the cave,

and behind the bookcase.

"I bet Billy took T-Rex home,"

Morgie said.

"And he didn't ask me!"

The next morning,

Morgie saw Billy.

"Where's T-Rex?" Morgie asked.

"I don't know," Billy said.

"I don't have him."

"Well, you better give him back," Morgie said.

And he walked away.

Morgie was mad at Billy.

Billy was mad at Morgie.

They didn't sit together

at story time.

They didn't play catch together.

They didn't share lunch.

They didn't even say good-bye!

"Why are you and Billy in a
fight?" Moffie asked.

"None of your business,"
Morgie snapped.

"Well, excuse me!" Moffie said.

"How was your day?"

Mama asked the twins.

"Morgie and Billy had a fight,"

Moffie said.

Mama said, "Well, I am

sure they will make up

and be friends again."

Morgie went outside.

"Want to go on the swing?"

Morgie asked Marcos.

"No, *gracias*. No, thank you,"

his little brother said.

Morgie went inside.

"Want to play dinosaurs?"

Morgie asked Moffie.

"No, thank you," Moffie said.

Morgie felt all alone.

He went to his room.

There on his bed was T-Rex!

Morgie hugged T-Rex.

"Where were you?"

Morgie asked.

Mama heard Morgie.

"I found T-Rex in Marcos's room.

He slept with T-Rex last night."

*Oh no!* thought Morgie.

Billy didn't take T-Rex

after all.

At dinner, Morgie told
everybody the whole story.
"Well," Papa said,
"you need to tell Billy
you are sorry."

Mama nodded.

"Then you will be friends again."

Morgie nodded.

This was going to be hard!

The next morning,

the twins saw Billy.

"Morgie has something to tell you,"

Moffie said.

"I'm sorry, Billy," Morgie said.

He told Billy everything.

"I feel really bad.

Can we be friends again?"

"Sure," Billy said.

It was after school.

Morgie and Billy were playing

with Morgie's dinosaurs.

"Gotcha!" Billy yelled.

"It's my cave now!"

Morgie and Billy laughed.